PRINCE NOT-S[...]

Once Upon a Prank

Roy L. Hinuss

Illustrated by Matt Hunt

[Imprint]
MAKE YOUR MARK

New York

[Imprint]
MAKE YOUR MARK

A part of Macmillan Publishing Group, LLC
175 Fifth Avenue, New York, NY 10010

PRINCE NOT-SO CHARMING: ONCE UPON A PRANK. Copyright © 2018 by
Imprint. All rights reserved. Printed in the United States of America by
LSC Communications, Harrisonburg, Virginia.

Library of Congress Control Number: 2017958060

ISBN 978-1-250-14238-2 (paperback) / ISBN 978-1-250-14237-5 (ebook)

Our books may be purchased in bulk for promotional, educational, or
business use. Please contact your local bookseller or the Macmillan
Corporate and Premium Sales Department at (800) 221-7945 ext. 5442 or
by e-mail at MacmillanSpecialMarkets@macmillan.com.

Book design by Ellen Duda

Illustrations by Matt Hunt

Imprint logo designed by Amanda Spielman

First edition, 2018

1   3   5   7   9   10   8   6   4   2

mackids.com

You stole this book? Oh no! For shame!
Now we have to curse your name.
May your days see stormy weather.
May your ears get tied together.
May your feet smell like old cheese.
May you catch some gross disease.
May you get a paper cut.
And may a jester zap your butt.

For Alex, my jester-in-training

PRiNCE NOT·SO CHARMiNG

The Prince Not-So Charming series

Once Upon a Prank

Her Royal Slyness

CHAPTER 1

Prince Carlos Charles Charming jingle-jangled down the twisty corridors of Fancy Castle. His eyes squinted in concentration. His lips silently repeated his routine over and over.

Tumble, juggle, dance a jig.

Booger gag, then flip your wig.

Tumble, juggle, dance a jig.

Booger gag, then flip your wig.

"Okay, I got this." He nodded, and the bells on his three-pointed hat tinkled. "I'll be great."

But Carlos repeated his routine a few more times, just to make sure.

He slowly turned the corner, careful to keep his hat quiet. He peeked through an enormous doorway and into the throne room.

The throne room wasn't a room, really. It was more like a very long and very large stone hallway. But it was an *impressive* hallway, with a high, pointy ceiling that looked like it

belonged in a church. The walls were lined
with dozens of portraits of the many, many
generations of the Charming family.

Some of the portraits showed Charmings
admiring the natural beauty of Faraway
Kingdom.

Others showed Charmings riding horses.

Most of them, however, showed Charmings stabbing things. Charmings loved to get stabby.

And every Charming in every portrait looked brave and noble and serious.

Oh, so serious.

Ugh.

A ribbon of red carpet stretched from the doorway to the far wall. The far wall was *very* far, about a hundred feet away. There, seated upon a golden throne, was Carlos's dad, King Carmine.

Poor Dad, Carlos thought. *He works too hard.*

Carlos was right. The king worked all the time. He even skipped meals when there was too much work to do. And there was *always* too much work to do. The man was little more than skin and bones.

The king had been working in his throne room since dawn, shuffling through paperwork and signing his name on each page with a floppy peacock quill. Even from a hundred feet away, Carlos had no trouble making out his father's frown.

King Carmine was a good king. He was also a good dad; he was always loving and patient with Carlos. And they shared the same

light tan skin and friendly dark brown eyes. But that frown! It was always on his face. Carlos had to think very, very hard to remember the last time his dad had laughed.

But today, Carlos was going to change all that. He was going to turn that royal frown upside down. He sucked in a deep breath.

"ARE YOU READY TO LAUGH?!" he bellowed, his words bouncing off the throne-room walls.

The startled king jerked his head up from his paperwork.

"I SAAAAAID, ARE YOU READY TO LAUGH?!" Carlos yelled.

The king's eyes fell back to the stack of

papers in his lap. "Carlos, can you do this later? I'm really busy, son."

"IS THAT A YES?!" Carlos screamed.

"It is *not* a yes," the king said.

"YOU SAID 'YES!' SO PREPARE YOURSELF FOR THE MIRTH-MAKING MERRIMENT OF THE FANTASTICALLY FABULOUS FUNNYMAN! THE ONE... THE ONLY... YOUR SON... THE GREAT COMI-CARLOS!"

Carlos leapt through the throne room's doorway. His stomach trembled with nervous delight, making the bells on his lime-green jester pants happily jingle. His routine was etched into his memory. It was a part of him now.

Tumble, juggle, dance a jig.

Booger gag, then flip your wig.

First: tumbling. Carlos tucked himself into a perfect somersault, performed a quick roll down the red carpet, and sprang back up onto his feet.

"Ta-da!"

It was a super somersault, perhaps his best ever. But there was a problem.

For weeks, Carlos had rehearsed his routine in his tiny bedroom. There, a single somersault would move him from one end

of the room to the other. After the somersault, he would move on to the second part
of his routine: juggling.

Carlos's one somersault didn't get him to
the other end of *this* room, however. His dad
was still ninety feet away.

Hm, he thought. *I need to get closer. I better
somersault again.*

He tucked, rolled, and, again, sprang to
his feet.

"Ta-da!"

Now Dad was about eighty feet away.

Dang.

So Carlos performed another somersault.

Tuck! Roll! Spring!

Seventy feet.

Tuck! Roll! Spring!

The last somersault was a little wobbly but still sort of good.

Sixty feet.

Carlos couldn't tell if his somersaults were improving his dad's mood, because they were starting to make him a little dizzy.

"Carlos!" the king yelled.

Nope, he still sounds frowny, Carlos thought. *He needs to see more somersaults.*

Carlos stumbled a little as he got ready.

Tuck! Roll! Sort of spring!

Fifty feet.

Tuck! Roll . . .

. . . SPLAT!

Carlos patted his pants pocket. The eggs he had planned to juggle were now an icky, sticky mess.

"Ugh." His dizzy brain made the room tilt sideways.

Let me think. Let me think. What comes next?

Tumble, juggle . . . Tumble, juggle . . .

"Dance a jig!" Carlos exclaimed. "It's time to dance a jig!"

"Carlos," the king said, "not now. No jigs."

Carlos skipped and pranced, stumbling a bit because he was still dizzy. Egg yolk soaked through his pants, dribbled down his leg, and formed a gooey puddle at his feet—a puddle that he slipped in.

"YIKES!" Carlos thudded to the floor.

The king gasped. "Carlos!" He stood in alarm. The high stack of papers that had been resting on his lap whooshed out and fluttered across the floor. "Are you all right?"

"Yeah," Carlos panted. "Did you find my fall funny?"

"No!" the king said. "I thought you hurt yourself!"

"Oh, no," Carlos said. "*You're* the one who is going to get hurt! You're going to hurt yourself *laughing* when you hear my joke!"

"Carlos." The king rubbed his eyes. "No jokes, please."

Carlos struggled to sit up, more determined than ever. "One joke?"

"No," the king said.

"Just one," Carlos said. "Just one joke."

"No." The king's eyes drifted to the scattered papers at his feet. "Oh, what a mess."

"Please?" Carlos asked. "Just one. You'll like it. I promise."

The king was too unsettled by the mess to put up a fight. In addition to being a good king, he was a tidy king. He stammered, "I-I really . . . I really need to pick up these papers, son."

"Pleeeeease!" Carlos begged. "One little

joke! You'll really like it, Dad. You'll laugh so much. Pleeeeeeeeeeeeease."

The king sighed as he spoke, making his voice kind of whispery. "Okay," he whisper-sighed. "One joke."

"What's the difference between a booger and a peanut-butter sandwich?" Carlos asked.

"What?" the king replied.

"I said . . ." Carlos began to answer.

"I *heard* what you said." The king's eyebrows knitted together. Now he had frowny lines on his forehead that matched the frown on his mouth.

"Do you know?" Carlos asked. "Do you

know the difference between a booger and a peanut-butter sandwich? Do you?"

"No," the king said.

"You don't know the difference?!" Carlos gasped, sounding alarmed. "Remind me never to have lunch at your house! HA-HA!"

The king didn't laugh. Instead, he carefully tiptoed through the piles of papers down the red carpet. He stopped at the edge of the puddle of eggs, where Carlos sat. He offered his hand. Carlos took it, and the king pulled the boy to his feet.

"So, um . . ." Carlos cleared his throat and rubbed an achy elbow. He must have banged it when he slipped. "Did you like my routine?"

"Carlos . . ." the king began.

"Did you like *any* of it?" Carlos asked, nervously peering down at his curly toed shoes.

"Son . . ." the king began again.

"I just wanted to try to make you happy," Carlos said.

The lines on the king's forehead faded. His eyes grew wider. Kinder. "You *do* make me happy," he said. "But you know how your mother and I feel about this. You cannot be a jester. You are a *prince*. You have a responsibility to serve this kingdom *as* a prince. You need to do princely things."

"But, Dad, I don't want to do princely things," Carlos said. "I want to be funny. I want to do fun-ly things."

"*Fun-ly* is not a word." The king adjusted his crown. He plucked a piece of lint from his fur cloak. "Carlos, you and I are Charmings." With a grand gesture, the king swept his hand at the dozens of portraits that hung from the walls. "For two thousand years, Charmings have ruled Faraway Kingdom. I am following in this grand tradition. Do you know why?"

Carlos's chin dropped to his chest. "Because it is your duty."

The king nodded. "My Charming duty."

At that moment, a poop joke popped into Carlos's head, but he kept it to himself.

"And someday you, too, will be king," Carlos's father said. "And to be a king, you must first learn how to be a prince. And that means . . . ?"

". . . doing princely things," Carlos sighed.

"That's right, son," the king said. "So I need you to run downstairs and get fitted for a suit of armor."

"Armor?!" Carlos sputtered. "But . . ."

"Please." Carlos's dad was so nice that even his kingly orders were polite.

"Okay," Carlos replied, but he said it in a way that showed it *wasn't* okay. Not okay *at all*.

Carlos thumped back to the entrance of the throne room, keeping his eyes on the floor so he could avoid any egg puddles. The king began to scoop up his paperwork.

"Dad?" Carlos said.

"Yes, son," the king answered.

"Before I go, can I do the last part of my routine?"

The king's eyes grew wide. "There's *more?*"

Carlos nodded. "**Tumble, juggle, dance a jig. Booger gag, then flip your wig**. I did everything but the wig-flipping part."

"What's the wig-flipping part?" the king asked.

"My hat," Carlos said. "I throw it really high in the air, and it lands back on my head. It's pretty cool. I practiced it for a long time."

The king nodded. "All right. Go ahead."

"Really?" Carlos asked.

"Yes," the king said. "Do your trick."

"WOO!" Carlos triumphantly yanked off his jester hat and hurled it high up in the air.

He braced himself for his routine's dazzling finish.

But the hat never came back down.

Carlos's and the king's eyes rose heavenward. The hat was tangled in the chandelier.

"Dang it," Carlos said.

The corners of King Carmine's mouth twitched a bit into something approaching a smile but didn't quite get there.

"You're lucky," the king said.

"I am?" Carlos didn't feel lucky at all.

The king nodded. "Those chandelier candles are usually lit. You're lucky the lamplighter quit yesterday." The king's mouth twitched again. "Your hat could've gone up in flames."

CHAPTER 2

Prince Carlos Charles Charming clinked and clunked down the castle hallway. He reached a plain wooden door with rusty hinges and opened it slightly. It made a creaking sound. Inside, lying on a raggedy bed of straw, was perhaps the happiest man in Faraway Kingdom.

"Carlos, my boy!" Jack the Jester shouted with joy. "Good news! The new Hammacher Jester catalog arrived today!" He riffled through the catalog's pages with the eagerness of a puppy. "Look at this! A jewel-encrusted whoopee cushion! Fake vomit made by Bavarian artisans! And . . ."

Jack was so excited by the cool stuff on each page that it took him a few moments to notice how Carlos was dressed. The old man's smile faded. "Dear goodness, young'un. Why are you wearing that?"

Carlos was clad from head to toe in an iron suit so heavy and hot that he could barely stand up.

"Dad's making me wear it," Carlos said.

Jack sprang to his feet. He was an old man, but many years of tumbling, juggling, and dancing jigs had made him as nimble as a ballerina. The dark brown skin of his face was wrinkled with laugh lines. And, at this moment, frown lines. "Well, that's ridiculous! Jesters can't tumble, juggle, and dance jigs in armor! There's not enough mobility, son! Your dad is a good king—a *very* good king—but he doesn't understand jestering. I'll have a talk with him about this armor business."

Carlos sighed miserably. "Dad is making me wear armor because he doesn't *want* me to be a jester."

Jack's smile melted away. "Oh, I see," he said. "So I guess we'll need to reschedule your stilt-walking lesson."

"I guess so." Carlos's throat tightened. "Dad says I need to be more of a prince. It's my duty."

"Heh heh. Doody." Because he was a jester, Jack always thought of the word *doody* whenever he heard *duty*. His chuckle, however, was halfhearted at best. Soon the old man's mouth stretched into a proud, determined straight line. "Let me show you something."

Jack scampered to a hefty wooden chest, flung open the lid, and dug around inside. By the time he found what he was looking for, the floor of his room was littered with chattering teeth, rubber chickens, and googly-eyed glasses.

"Take a look at these!" Jack expertly fanned out a stack of trading cards. Each card featured a portrait of a colorful jester.

Some of the portraits showed jesters balancing on balls.

Others showed jesters riding pigs.

Most of them, however, showed jesters squirting things with water. Jesters loved to get squirty.

And *every* jester in *every* portrait wore a joyous, impish smile.

Carlos couldn't help but smile back.

"See these?" Jack said. "These are my merry, mischievous ancestors. For two thousand years, members of my family have spread joy in castles, under circus tents, and at birthday parties. I am following in their jingle-toed footsteps. Do you know why?"

Carlos's smile faded. He knew the answer to Jack's question but didn't respond.

"Say it," Jack said.

"Duty," Carlos mumbled.

"Say it correctly!" Jack demanded.

"*Doooody*," Carlos said.

"Yessir!" Jack sprang onto his bed,

stretched out his arms, and spoke as if he were addressing a crowd of thousands. "Making people laugh is the world's most honorable profession! A laughing world is a happier world! A more peaceful world! A jolly, jelly-belly, silly world!"

Then Jack let out an alarming shout: "CARLOS! THINK FAST!"

A spray of water squirted from the flower pinned to Jack's shirt. But Carlos had learned from his months of jester training. He effortlessly deflected the water with his shield.

Jack nodded with satisfaction. "Nice reflexes, kiddo."

Normally a compliment from Jack would fill Carlos with joy, but not today.

"I *want* to make people laugh," Carlos sighed. "I've wanted to make people laugh ever since I heard my first fart joke."

"I told it to you when you were four years old," Jack said. "Even at that age, I could see you had the soul of a jester. You had a little twinkle in your eye." Jack smiled at the memory. "Do you remember the joke?"

"Why did the teacher fart in the empty classroom?" Carlos asked.

"Because she was a private *tooter*!" Jack boomed.

And, just like old times, the two forgot their troubles and laughed themselves silly.

But their laughs were cut short when Carlos's mom, Queen Cora, burst through the doorway. She was a big woman with an even bigger personality. She was perhaps the second happiest person in Faraway Kingdom. A smile spread across her tan face from ear to ear.

"Oh, there you are!" She clasped her hands together in delight. "Let me get a look at my little knight in shining armor! Is the suit uncomfortable anywhere?"

"It's uncomfortable *everywhere*," Carlos said.

But the queen didn't hear Carlos's complaint. She had a hard time hearing *anything* when she was excited. She was often excited. And now, she was *very* excited.

"Oh, you are so handsome!" She gave Carlos a big bear hug. His armor rattled in protest. "You will be the most handsome dragon slayer in all the land!"

"Dragon slayer?" Jack sputtered.

"Dmmun slmmph?" Carlos sputtered. (His face was smushed into his mom's shoulder.)

"What was that, honey?" the queen asked.

"Mmmuphuh!" Carlos said.

"You must speak up, dear," the queen said. "Princes shouldn't mumble."

"Your Majesty," Jack interrupted. "I believe that your kind words have taken the prince's breath away!"

"Hm? Oh, deary my!" The queen released her son from her smothery, motherly hug. "So sorry. Yes, honey?"

Carlos gasped for air. "Dragon . . . (gasp) . . . slayer? (wheeze) I can't . . . (cough cough) . . . kill a dragon."

Cora fluttered her fingers as if to shoo away such a silly remark. "Of course you can!"

"But I've never used a sword!" Carlos said. "I've never even *seen* a dragon!"

But the queen didn't hear him. "Oh, this is so exciting! I'm so excited! You must be so excited, Carlos! Are you excited? Of course you are! For thousands of years Charmings have slayed dragons! And you will follow in their grand tradition! At last, you will do what comes naturally to you!"

"Fart jokes are what come naturally to me," Carlos said.

His comment made the queen lose the thread of the conversation. "Hm? What? Jokes?" She chuckled a bit. "Oh, no, honey, you don't tell *jokes* to dragons—you *slay* them. But don't worry, you'll learn. You will be trained to fight." The queen trembled with delight. "In fact, you are very, very lucky!"

"I am?" Carlos didn't feel lucky at all.

"Yes!" The queen was so excited that she began to hop up and down. She became very jiggly. "Because you are going to be trained by your best friend, Gilbert the Gallant!"

Gilbert the Gallant was *not* Carlos's best friend. Not even close.

"More like Gilbert the Goofus," he muttered. This day just kept getting worse and worse.

The queen didn't hear Carlos's "goofus"

remark. "I know!" she cried. "I am just as ex-cited as you are! I am so glad you two are so close. Gilbert will be a very good princely influence on you. Did you know that Gilbert the Gallant was named *Peasant* magazine's Princeliest Prince Alive?"

"Yes," Carlos said. "You told me."

"I did?" the queen asked.

"Many times," Carlos said.

"Then you're as excited as I am!" The queen snapped open a silk fan and made it flutter in front of her face. Excitement some-times makes people sweaty. "Well! Anyway! Gilbert is waiting for you in the courtyard right now! So! Let's get you set up! Let's turn you into a prince! Let's make you the Prince-liest Prince Alive!"

The queen clapped her hands three times. At once, a swarm of servants thundered into the room, each bearing a weapon. Soon Carlos's arms were piled high with swords, daggers, maces, bows, and arrows. His armor squeaked and creaked under the weight of it all.

"There!" the queen said. "Have fun! And don't forget to get stabby!" She spun on her heel to leave but stopped at the doorframe. She faced her son once again and gave him a long, admiring look.

"You are so big," the queen said. "So brave." Her voice quivered as a happy tear formed in the corner of her eye. "I am so, so very proud of you."

"Thanks, Mom." Carlos felt his ears get hot.

Then, in a flurry of silk, Queen Cora swooshed away down the hall.

CHAPTER 3

"Keep the tip of your sword up, Carlos," Gilbert the Gallant said. "You're slaying dragons, not salamanders."

Gilbert chuckled at his little joke.

Carlos didn't. *Leave the jokes to the professionals,* he thought.

Gilbert the Gallant, the soon-to-be-king

of nearby Ever-After Land, was everything Carlos wasn't: tall, muscular, poised, and proper. He also walked around in his armor as if it were as comfortable as a bathrobe.

How can Gilbert stand wearing this tin tuxedo? Carlos wondered. He fidgeted and twitched as pointy bits of metal jabbed his back, front, sides, arms, legs, and left butt cheek.

Gilbert always wore armor, but he never bothered with a helmet. That would hide his sly, knowing smile. Aside from stabbing things, Gilbert's favorite hobby was smiling slyly and knowingly.

A helmetless head also showed off Gilbert's handsome face; flawless, ebony skin;

and elegant nose, which looked as if it were always smelling something wonderful. (And Gilbert's nose usually was, for fair maidens regularly offered him flowers.)

Gilbert the Gallant's most striking feature, however, were his eyes, which were deep, dark, and confident. Gilbert was always confident in his princely abilities. And, today, he was confident that he could turn Carlos into a prince, too.

But Carlos was not confident that he could become a prince. And the longer he trained with Gilbert, the less confident he became.

"Raise your sword, and let's try again,"

Gilbert said. He also possessed the princely trait of patience. "Keep the blade up, now. Pay attention to that."

Carlos *was* paying attention. At least, he was trying to. The reason his blade kept tilting toward the weeds was because it was so dang heavy. How was he supposed to slay anything with a sword he could hardly lift?

"All right, then," Gilbert said. He effortlessly raised his own sword and positioned his feet just so. "Come at me, and I will do my best to defend myself. Aim for my heart. Show no mercy."

Carlos took a deep breath and steadied

himself. *Stab Gilbert's heart,* he thought. *Got it.*

Carlos wished he had a squirting flower woven into his chain mail. An unexpected spray of water into Gilbert's eyes would be useful right about now.

Unfortunately, Carlos had nothing to rely on but his sword.

Using both hands, he lifted the blade, pointing the tip as best he could in the direction of Gilbert's armor-covered heart. Carlos's arm muscles trembled under the weight.

The rest of Carlos trembled, too, but for a different reason.

He was trembling with anger.

He was angry that his dad was forcing him to be a prince. Angry that he had to kill a dragon. Angry that his sword was so heavy. Angry that he had to spend the afternoon with stupid, perfect Gilbert. Angry

that his armor poked and stabbed him every which way. Angry that his jester hat was still stuck in the chandelier. And angry that he was hot and tired and busy and bored—*all at the same time.*

Never in his life had Carlos felt stabbier.

He furrowed his eyebrows and focused on his target with the intensity of a laser.

"Aim right for my heart, Carlos," Gilbert said.

"Oh," Carlos replied through gritted teeth, "don't you worry."

It was now or never.

ATTACK!

This is what happened next:

1. With a determined roar, Carlos lunged.

2. With little effort, Gilbert swatted his sword away.

3. Without further prompting, the sword leapt from Carlos's hands, soared through the air in a beautiful arc, and, with a stout **CHUNK!**, stuck into the ground some ten feet away.

The two princes regarded the faraway sword for a long, uncomfortable moment.

"Um . . . better!" Gilbert said finally, wearing a smile that didn't quite match the look

in his eyes. "Much better than last time. Yes. Very good, Carlos. *Very* good."

Gilbert cleared his throat and continued, "Perhaps, however, the broadsword is not *exactly* the right weapon for you."

Earlier in the lesson, Gilbert had come to the same conclusion about the mace, the bow, the dagger, and the quarterstaff.

"So!" Gilbert said. "Shall we give the hatchet a try, then?"

"I'm afraid there's no time for that," a distant voice said.

Carlos and Gilbert turned toward Fancy Castle to find King Carmine leaning out of an upper window. "How is the training coming along, Gilbert the Gallant?"

Gilbert bowed to the distant figure. "Very well, Your Majesty. Your son is a quick study."

"Excellent," the king said. "I need to put his skills into practice. A dragon has been spotted in the Somewhat-Enchanted Forest. Carlos, will you be a good boy and go out and slay it for me?"

Carlos's armor rattled in alarm. "Wait. What?!"

"I need you to slay the dragon, please," the king said.

"I can't slay a dragon!" Carlos's voice suddenly became shrill, squeaky, and unfamiliar. "I've only trained for one day! And I can't do anything!" He pointed an accusing finger at Gilbert. "He'll tell you! He's trained me on five weapons so far, and I stink at all of them!"

Gilbert, in his elegant, polite, and princely way, supported Carlos's position. "Prince Carlos could, perhaps, benefit from a bit more training, Your Majesty."

"There is a beast lurking in the forest, Prince Gilbert," the king said. "It is not going to wait for Carlos to finish his training. A properly motivated dragon can torch a hundred villages in a single day. Carlos needs to go now."

"NOW?!" Carlos shouted. His head filled with a jumble of panicked, jostling shouts. *This is ridiculous! I'm supposed to be a jester! I'm supposed to be practicing stilt-walking and card tricks and playing pop-song parodies on the lute! I can't slay a dragon! I'll be killed! Roasted alive! Turned into an appetizer! Doesn't Dad understand that? Doesn't he care?!*

Carlos didn't *say* any of these things, but King Carmine seemed able to read the boy's mind.

"Son," the king said, "I know how frightened you must feel. I was frightened when I fought my first dragon. My father was frightened when he fought *his* first dragon. As was his father. And his father's father. And so on. But we fought through that fear, Carlos. All of us. And you will, too. As a prince, you must protect the subjects of Faraway Kingdom."

Then the king added, "It is your duty. Your Charming duty."

Unfortunately, Carlos was too upset to think of poop jokes at a time like this.

CHAPTER 4

Pushing a wheelbarrow piled high with weapons, Carlos slowly, achingly, began to roll his way toward the Somewhat-Enchanted Forest.

King Carmine was there to see his boy off. "Are you sure you don't want to ride Cornelius?" he asked.

Cornelius was the royal horse.

"No. I'd rather walk," Carlos said.

Carlos didn't *really* want to walk. He just didn't want to be alone with Cornelius. Last week, he had tried out his new hand buzzer on the horse's backside, and Cornelius had been giving him the stink eye ever since. Cornelius clearly had revenge on his mind.

Better to walk, Carlos thought. *Better safe than sorry.*

"All right," the king replied, a bit uncertain. "Just watch out for quicksand."

This stopped Carlos and his wheelbarrow in their tracks. "Quicksand?"

The king nodded. "The Somewhat-Enchanted Forest is loaded with it. Cornelius knows how to avoid it, if you want to reconsider...."

Peering over the king's shoulder, Carlos spotted Cornelius leaning out of his barn stall. Their eyes met.

Oh, you will pay for buzzing my butt, the horse's eyes seemed to say. *You will paayyyyy.*

"I'll stick with the wheelbarrow," Carlos said.

"Oh, my brave boy!" Queen Cora said.

She was also there to see Carlos off. She dabbed happy, sad, and proud tears from her cheeks with a monogrammed hankie. "Give your mother a big hug!"

"Does the hug have to be big?" Carlos asked.

It did. Carlos disappeared into her loving, suffocating arms.

"Oh, this is so exciting!" she cried (while crying).

"Mmmpfh," Carlos replied.

Carlos had hardly gone a hundred yards before he regretted not taking Cornelius. Whatever revenge the horse had in mind couldn't have been worse than wrestling a wheelbarrow through the forest. Every step was an ordeal. Carlos leaned into the wheelbarrow, doing his best to muscle it over the thousands of rocks and roots that studded the ground. Carlos was sweating so much that he was convinced his armor would be rusty by sundown.

"I can't do this," he muttered.

As he shoved the wheelbarrow forward inch by inch, a plan formed in Carlos's mind:

He would select one weapon from the wheelbarrow and leave everything else behind. It was the only way he'd be able to keep going.

I'll take the hatchet, he thought. It was the only weapon in the wheelbarrow that he hadn't trained with. In other words, it was the only weapon he might not stink at using. He *probably* did, but he *might* not. So the hatchet it would be.

Just as Carlos was about to put his plan into action, however, the forest became more accommodating. The path grew smooth and sloped gently downward, pulling the wheelbarrow forward. All Carlos had to do was steer.

His pace quickened. His mood lightened. His mind shifted to a happier place. He watched the squirrels dance and scamper wildly in the treetops. He listened to the playful chirps of songbirds. He took a moment to enjoy the *crish-crish* sound of his feet stepping on dry leaves.

What struck Carlos most, however, were the trees. Standing tall and straight, they soared into the sky, their topmost branches disappearing into the clouds. He'd had no idea that trees could grow so high. And there were *thousands* of them, row upon row, like an army of soldiers.

Or, perhaps, like a captive audience.

A smile crept across Carlos's face.

"Good evening, ladies and ferns!" he announced. "You wanna hear a joke about paper? Ah, never mind—that joke is *tear*-able!"

Carlos noticed that the clanking of his armor mixed with the *crish-crish* sound of the dry leaves sounded a lot like applause.

"Thank you, thank you!" he said. "Seriously, though, I really do appreciate all the paper you trees make. I love paper. I love books. I'm reading a great book now about the history of glue. I can't put it down!"

His armor clanked, the leaves crish-crished. Carlos bowed in appreciation.

"You're all too kind!" he said. "Here's another one: How many apples grow on a tree?"

He paused, as if he expected one of the oaks to shout out an answer.

"All of them!" he said. "HA-HA! We are rolling now!"

And, indeed, Carlos *was* rolling. He had

been so focused on telling jokes that he had failed to notice how the ground's gentle downward slope had become a rather steep hill. His slow stroll turned into a brisk walk and then a wild run.

"Whoa!" Carlos yelled. He dug his heels into the dirt, but gravity had taken over. The wheelbarrow wrenched itself from Carlos's grasp and lurched down the hill without him.

"Wait!" he shouted. "WAIT! STOP!"

The wheelbarrow, as if responding to Carlos's command, obeyed. It slowed down.

It wobbled and shuddered. After reaching the bottom of the hill, it skidded to a gentle stop.

None of the weapons had fallen out. Nothing was damaged.

Carlos let out a long, relieved sigh.

But then the ground beneath the wheelbarrow **blurbled** and **blorped**.

Quicksand! Carlos realized.

In an instant, the wheelbarrow, along with every sword, dagger, shield, mace, bow, arrow, quarterstaff, and hatchet in it, was swallowed by the earth.

The last item, Carlos's helmet, bobbed on the surface for a moment. The feather on top seemed to wave good-bye. Then it **blurble-blorped** into the quicksand, too.

"Oh, come ON!" Bubbling with frustration, Carlos folded his arms over his armored chest and stewed. *What now?* he

wondered. He couldn't come up with any-thing. He certainly couldn't be expected to slay a dragon after losing all his weapons. And his helmet. And a wheelbarrow.

All he could do at this point was . . .

Go home!

Carlos brightened. "Oh, that's a shame! But I have no choice!"

He turned on his armored heel and, with a merry **clank** and **clunk**, started back toward the castle.

Maybe this will teach Mom and Dad a lesson, he thought. The very idea gave Carlos an extra spring in his step. *They'll see that I'm not supposed to run around the woods hunting dragons. They'll see that I'm not supposed to be a prince. They'll finally understand that I'm meant to be a jester! They'll have no choice but to let me continue my training. They'll have no choice but to—*

Carlos awoke from his daydream with a start. A distant, unfamiliar sound had broken his concentration.

He paused and listened.

The distant sound repeated itself. But it wasn't so distant this time.

The sound was more distinct, too.

It was a roar.

A dragon's roar!

A chill of terror zipped up Carlos's spine.

CHAPTER 5

Carlos broke into a run.

CLANGITA BANGITA CLUNKITA CREAK-ITA CRASH!

Gah! He couldn't be noisier if he had a marching band strapped to his back.

Running in heavy armor couldn't be slower or more exhausting, either. Carlos had hardly begun his sluggish sprint before he stared to wheeze.

He needed to get rid of this stupid suit of armor once and for all.

Carlos **clanged**, **banged**, **clunked**, and **creaked**, half running and half crawling toward a cluster of boulders. It was as good a hiding place as any.

He flopped behind the largest boulder and landed on a bed of sharp stones. The armor protected him from injury, but it also thundered in protest, announcing his location to anything within shouting distance.

So much for hiding. Carlos could only hope that the dragon was hard of hearing.

He yanked off his iron gloves easily, but the thick leather straps that held his other armor in place were much more stubborn. Time and again he almost—*almost*—managed to get the buckles undone. But then his nervous hands would slip, the buckle would refasten itself, and he'd have to start all over again.

The sharp edge of the armor cut his index finger.

"Ow."

The straps pinched his pinkie.

"Ow."

He stubbed his ring finger.

"Ow."

He bent back the fingernail on his thumb.

"Ow!"

Then he cut, pinched, stubbed, and bent fingernail-ed his middle finger.

"OW!"

That last "ow" was much louder than it should've been.

He froze.

His ears searched for foreign sounds—footsteps along the path, the flapping of bat wings, a dragon's roar of rage. . . .

But all he heard was a whispery breeze blowing some leaves across the forest floor.

Could the dragon have lost interest?

Carlos listened some more.

Nothing. Even the breeze had silenced itself.

Could the dragon have been a figment of his imagination?

It was possible. He hadn't *seen* the dragon. He had only heard it.

And *had* he really heard it?

Maybe he was jumpy after losing all his weapons. And his helmet. And the wheelbarrow. The mind can play tricks on a jumpy person.

That's probably it, Carlos decided. *That's definitely it. I've been jumpy, and I heard a roar that wasn't really there.*

Then, suddenly—

ROAR!

That roar *was* really there.

The beastly snarl echoed off the trees and made the ground tremble like the skin of a drum. Carlos's attention flew back to the armor covering his arm. He managed to undo only one strap, but that made the armor loose enough for him to wriggle out the rest of the way.

The leather straps on his breastplate, however, were even trickier. These straps were tied together rather than buckled.

Oh, come on, Carlos thought. *Who triple-knotted this stupid thing?*

ROOOAAAR!

The dragon's bellow was so loud that Carlos hunched into a shivering ball. His head was between his knees. He was looking down at the bed of rocks he sat upon.

Lots of rocks.

Lots of *very sharp* rocks.

An idea forced its way into Carlos's jumbled, jumpy brain.

"Ha!" Carlos grabbed the sharpest rock in the bunch and hacked at the leather straps. Almost at once, the armor plates fell away. His body felt light and loose and eager to move.

He bolted from his hiding spot with a speed that he hadn't known he possessed.

His feet flew over roots, leaves, and stones. He leapt over tangles of shrubs. He skidded around the forest's majestic trees. And with every stride, he heard:

Jingle-jangle! Jingle-jangle!

Oh no! He had been wearing his jester clothes under the armor this whole time.

ROOOOOOAAAAAAAR!!

"No!" Carlos shrieked. "Leave me al—"

Before Carlos could finish the sentence, a shove from behind knocked him to the ground.

CHAPTER 6

Carlos lay facedown in the dirt, unable to move.

He felt the weight of the creature on his back. Its talons poked through the silk of his lime-green jester outfit.

This was it. The end. Carlos knew that much. All he could do was wait to be burned to a crisp or eaten alive. He hoped it wouldn't be as painful as it sounded.

Carlos felt the creature shift its weight and lean in close. He felt its fiery breath against the back of his neck.

"Oh, hai!" it said. "You the ice-cream man?"

Carlos coughed up a lungful of dirt. "Whuh?"

"I heard the jingle-jangles, and I wanna fudge-ickle," the creature said. "It cools my hot bref."

Carlos coughed some more. "I don't have any. . . . Can you . . . can you let me up, please?"

"Oh, sure, sure, sure!" the creature said. It stepped off his back.

Freed from the creature's weight, Carlos pulled himself into a sitting position.

Before him was a dragon. It looked exactly the way Carlos imagined a dragon would look. It had green-and-purple scales trimmed with orange highlights, a rubbery pair of bat wings on its back, a full set of sharp claws, and a long neck and tail. The only unexpected thing was the dragon's size. It was about the size of a sofa—a smallish one that can only sit two people (if their butts aren't too wide).

"I was calling you and calling you!" the dragon said. "Didn't you hear me?"

"That was you *calling*?" Carlos asked.

The dragon looked to its scaly feet with just a hint of guilt in its eyes. "I really wanna fudge-ickle," it explained. "And we're in the woods, so I don't need to use my indoor voice."

Carlos couldn't argue with that logic.

"Sorry about knocking you down, but you were about to go into the blurblings," the dragon said.

"Blurblings?" Carlos asked.

The dragon nodded. It picked up a rock and tossed it a few feet away from where Carlos sat. There it rested for the briefest of moments before the ground **blurbled** and **blorped** and pulled the rock under.

Quicksand! If Carlos had run just a few more steps, there would've been nothing left of him.

"Wow," Carlos said. "Thank you . . . um . . . Mr. Dragon."

"My name is Smudge," the dragon said. "I'm a little boy."

Carlos slowly held out his hand. "Nice to meet you, Smudge. I'm Carlos Charming."

"Carlos Charming?" Smudge repeated. "Hm. **Carrrrlos Charrrrming. Carrrrr-rrrrrrloooos** . . ." Smudge rolled the name over his tongue for a minute. It didn't seem to suit him. "CC. Can I call you CC?"

Before Carlos could reply, Smudge nodded, as if the matter was now settled. "I'll call you CC. You got a fudge-ickle?"

"No," Carlos said. "Sorry."

"Oh, poopers," Smudge harrumphed. "Oh, well. I still like you."

"I like you, too," Carlos replied. And he meant it. Smudge was cute. And sweet. And he had saved Carlos's life. There was a lot to like.

"I like ice cream. It makes my hot bref cold," Smudge said.

"Yeah, I remember you saying that," Carlos replied.

"Some dragons like to use their hot bref to set fire to villages and cook people alive, but not me," Smudge said. "I don't do that. So the other dragons call me a DINO."

"What's a DINO?" Carlos asked.

Smudge sighed sadly. "A Dragon In Name Only."

"Ah," Carlos said.

"So I come to the woods to do what I was meant to do." From behind his back, Smudge produced a half-finished scarf of red and green. "Knitting!"

"Wow," Carlos said. "I didn't know dragons knitted."

"They don't," Smudge sniffed. "But I do."

In that moment, Carlos's affection for the little dragon grew even stronger. After all, a dragon who knits is very much like a prince who jesters. Both Carlos and Smudge just wanted to live their lives in slightly unusual ways.

"And when I don't knit," Smudge said, "I look for the ice-cream man!"

"Does the ice-cream man ever come through the forest?" Carlos asked.

"No," Smudge pouted.

Carlos thought Smudge looked like he could use a pat on the nose. He was right.

"Oh, that feels pleas-ant!" Smudge said.

Carlos's eyes twinkled mischievously. "The reason you can't find the ice-cream man is because his ice-cream truck lost a wheel."

"It did?" Smudge asked.

Carlos nodded. "Yup. Do you know why?"

Smudge shook his head.

"Because of the rocky road!" Carlos said.

Smudge blinked.

"The ice-cream truck lost a wheel because of the *rocky road*," Carlos repeated.

This time, the dragon's eyes grew wide with understanding. "Rocky road is a kind of ice cream!"

"Yes," Carlos said.

Smudge began to pant with excitement. "And a *road* that is *rocky* can make an ice-cream truck break down!"

"Yes," Carlos said.

"THAT'S FUNNY!" And Smudge dissolved into a wave of snorting, tail-wagging, wing-flapping dragon giggles. "You're funny, CC!"

Carlos waited a moment, then asked, "Do you like juggling?"

Smudge's mouth dropped open. He bounced up and down. Merry bursts of smoke puffed from his nostrils.

"I'll take that as a yes." Carlos scooped three acorns off the ground and sent them flying through the air. Carlos was a very accomplished juggler, and he knew it. The many, many lonely nights of practicing in his bedroom were finally paying off.

Bop! He bounced an acorn off his elbow.

Bop! He bounced an acorn off his knee.

Klunk! He bounced an acorn off his head. Without missing a single toss, Carlos

crossed his eyes, staggered, and stumbled about as if the tiny acorn had knocked him senseless.

It was all part of the act, and Smudge went bananas for it.

The dragon flopped onto his back and wheezed with laughter. Enormous, gleeful fireballs rose up in the air.

"You know what?" Carlos asked, still juggling away.

"WHAT?!" Smudge could barely contain himself.

"I'm getting a little hungry!" Carlos tilted his head back and threw the acorns high up in the air.

PLOP! PLOP! PLOP! One by one, the acorns dropped into his open mouth.

Carlos grinned at Smudge, his cheeks as stuffed as a chipmunk's.

"BWAAAH!" The fire shooting from Smudge's mouth made the air shimmer and shake.

Carlos twisted his face into a mock grimace. "Bweh! Dese acowns taste tewwible!"

"THEY DO?!" Smudge was skipping in a circle now. He was too excited to sit still.

Carlos spat out the acorns with a **PTOO!** and resumed juggling.

More laughter. More fireballs.

Smudge was having the time of his life. So was Carlos.

In fact, both Smudge and Carlos were having *such* a wonderful time that neither noticed the distant, ominous rumble of hoofbeats.

CHAPTER 7

"CARLOS! GET DOWN!"

Startled, Carlos dropped one of his acorns. "Dang. Wait—what?"

A horse and rider burst through a distant tangle of shrubbery.

The horse was Cornelius. The rider was—

"Gilbert!" Carlos shouted. "What are you doing here?"

Cornelius reared up on his hind legs. Gilbert smiled, revealing a set of perfectly straight teeth. Even from a distance, Carlos was blinded by their whiteness.

The proud prince unsheathed his sword and raised it in triumph above his head. The blade glinted in the late-afternoon sun. It was even more blinding than his teeth, if that was even possible.

"I'M HERE TO SAVE YOU FROM THAT VICIOUS, FIRE-BREATHING DRAGON!" Gilbert declared. He spurred Cornelius forward into an earth-shaking gallop.

"NO! STOP!" Carlos ran toward the racing horse and rider to catch them, to slow them down, to do *anything*. His legs churned as fast as they could go. He waved his fists in the air. (These weren't fists of fury; Carlos was making fists because he was still thoughtlessly holding an acorn in each hand.) "THAT DRAGON IS MY FRIEND!"

But Gilbert and Cornelius were too wrapped up in their princely and horsely duties to listen. They spotted the small, curious dragon, and their killing instincts kicked in. They barreled past Carlos, heading straight for Smudge.

"WAIT!" Carlos screamed at Gilbert's and Cornelius's backs.

But they didn't wait.

Gilbert leveled his sword.

Smudge, now aware of the danger storming toward him, let out a sound. It was a sound that was very different from the throaty roars that had sent Carlos running or the laughs that had later filled Carlos with joy.

The sound was shrill.

Piercing.

Frightened.

It was a scream. **"AAAAAAHHHH!"**

The scream echoed in Carlos's ears and lit a fire inside his brain. He scanned his surroundings for a weapon. Finding nothing but what was already in his hands, he hurled the acorns at his targets as hard as he could.

One acorn smacked Gilbert on the back of his helmetless head. The other pegged Cornelius in the butt.

Gilbert wobbled a little and drooped to one side. Cornelius bucked and leapt and launched Gilbert from his saddle.

A moment later, Gilbert was flat on his back, separated from his sword. Cornelius thundered through the underbrush and back toward the castle, the rhythm of his hoofbeats fading away.

"What the . . . ?" Gilbert mumbled, his words a little slurred. He blinked his confident eyes, which looked a little less confident than usual. In fact, they were a wee bit crossed. His gaze landed upon his sword just in time to watch the earth swallow it up with a **blurble** and a **blorp**.

"Are you okay, Gilbert?" Carlos asked.

"What . . . what hit me?" Gilbert asked.

"An acorn. I hit Cornelius, too." Suddenly, the recent hand-buzzer incident

flashed into Carlos's mind. "Man, that horse is going to kill me."

Gilbert shook off a bit of his dizziness and raised himself onto his elbows.

"You felled Cornelius and me with *acorns*?" Gilbert asked.

Carlos nodded.

"While we were at a full gallop?" Gilbert asked.

Carlos nodded.

"At the *same time*?" Gilbert asked.

Carlos nodded a third time.

Gilbert quickly looked around to make sure no one else had seen his fall. No one had.

"How did you *do* all that?" he asked.

"I'm a jester," Carlos replied, his chest swelling a bit. "Jesters juggle. And juggling jesters throw with great accuracy."

"I suppose so," Gilbert said.

"Now, I have a question for you." Carlos's expression grew hard. "What are you doing here?"

Gilbert rubbed the raw spot on the back of his head and sat up. "Your father sent me."

"What?" Carlos asked. "Why?"

Gilbert looked uncertain. "After you went into the forest with your wheelbarrow, I took the king aside and explained that our lessons hadn't gone very well."

Carlos's face flushed. What Gilbert had said was true, of course, but Carlos still felt insulted. He was insulted that Gilbert and his dad were talking about him behind his back. He was insulted that his father sent Gilbert to watch over him like a babysitter. He was insulted by the *sneakiness* of it all.

"You and my dad both stink," he said.

"No!" Gilbert said. "Your father was worried about you! I was, too. So he asked me to follow you. He instructed me to keep out of sight and not get involved unless you were in real trouble. So when I saw the fireballs, I thought— **OOF!**"

Gilbert didn't think **OOF. OOF** was the

sound Gilbert made when Smudge jumped

on him, sending him sprawling back onto

the ground.

"Oh, hai!" Smudge was, once again, his

old cheerful self. He wasn't one to let an

attempted murder get in the way of a new friendship. "Are you the ice-cream man?"

Clearly, some introductions were in order.

"Gilbert, this is Smudge," Carlos said. "Smudge, meet Gilbert."

"Hai." Smudge extended his paw.

Gilbert paused for a moment. He was struggling with the idea that he was making the acquaintance of a dragon. Then he paused some more to note the sharp talons on Smudge's paw. Finally, he cautiously accepted it.

Smudge rolled the new name over his tongue. "Gilbert. Gilbert? **Gilllllllllberrrrrrt**.

Hm. **Giiiiiiiiilbeeeeeeeert**. Hm." Smudge twisted his mouth into a thoughtful grimace. "Can I call you Gert?"

"No," Gilbert said.

"Gert." Smudge nodded. As far as the dragon was concerned, the matter was settled. "I don't fireball people, Gert. I knit. See?" He held up his scarf.

"I thought I saw fireballs," Gilbert said.

"You did. Those were laughs," Carlos explained.

"Laughs?" Gilbert asked.

"Biiiiig laughs!" Smudge corrected.

"I did a comedic juggling bit," Carlos explained.

"CC is so funny, Gert," Smudge said. "Soooo funny. I laughed soooooo hard!" The memory of Carlos's routine brought out more laughs and a few tiny fireballs. "CC slayed me!"

Carlos's eyebrows went up. "I *slayed* you?" he asked. "I *did* slay you, didn't I?"

"Yes, indeedy," Smudge replied.

CHAPTER 8

"That is not the kind of slaying I had in mind," King Carmine said. "And I think you know that."

The king slumped in his throne. He looked a bit more tired than usual, and he always looked sort of tired.

"Yeah, I know," Carlos admitted. "But the slaying I did is a lot harder than the slaying you wanted me to do."

Smudge nodded. His forked tongue slurped up the last dribbles of his fudge-sickle. "CC's right. Dragons don't like jokes so much."

The king looked at Smudge and then back at Carlos. Then the king rubbed his eyes as if they hurt. "Okay, fine—you slayed a dragon. Good job."

Carlos wanted to say "Oh, and don't forget: I *also* defeated Prince Gilbert the Perfect on the field of battle!"

Before he could, however, the king spoke once more. "I'm glad you're safe, son. And I'm sorry that I underestimated you."

That made Carlos forget what he wanted to say.

"That's okay," he replied after a moment. And he was telling the truth. It really *was* okay.

"And CC has *more* good news!" Smudge had finished his ice cream and was now fully part of the conversation.

"It's true," Carlos said. "I do have more good news."

The king sank a little lower in his throne. "Oh, geez, what is it?"

"I hired you a new lamplighter!" Carlos said.

"You did?" the king asked. "Who?" Then he figured it out. "Wait—no! We are not keeping a dragon in the castle!"

"Why not?" Carlos protested.

"Because he is a *dragon*!" the king said. "They are not safe! And he is— **OOF!**"

The king didn't say the dragon was **OOF**.
The **OOF** was because Smudge leapt onto the
king, nearly knocking him off his throne.

"Oh, I am safe," Smudge assured him
with a smile. "And I made you a scarf!"

Before the king could protest, Smudge wrapped the knitted creation around the king's way-too-skinny neck. "I'm also a good worker! Watch!"

Smudge flapped his bat wings. It took some effort for him to get off the ground; flying was clearly not his strong suit. But before long, he was dangling from one of the many chandeliers in the throne room. With a gentle puff of dragon breath, he lit a candle. With another puff, he lit the candle beside it. Then the next one. And the next one. On and on he went, until the entire chandelier was completely, merrily aglow.

"See that?" Carlos's smile was as wide as

could be. "Smudge can light the candles faster than anyone! He doesn't need a ladder. *And* you can pay him in ice cream."

"Ice cream cools my hot bref!" Smudge called down from the rafters.

The king wavered. "Well, um . . . I don't know. . . ."

"Mom loves him," Carlos added.

"She met the dragon?" the king asked.

Carlos nodded. "She saw us come in. She said it would be exciting to have a dragon around the castle."

The king rolled his eyes. "That sounds like something she'd say."

Smudge gently rocked in the chandelier,

as if it were a porch swing. "I'll knit you a sweater!"

"Okay, okay," the king whisper-sighed. "He can stay."

"Smudge!" Carlos shouted to the ceiling. "Dad said okay! You can light the other chandeliers!"

"No, I can't," the dragon replied. "There's a jingle hat in this one."

"Oh, right!" Carlos said. "Drop it down to me!"

Smudge did. Carlos took a running leap to a very particular point in the middle of the throne room. As if on cue, the hat plopped directly onto Carlos's head.

The jester-in-training dropped to his knees and stretched out his arms in triumph. "TA-DA!"

King Carmine smiled. It was not a smile of amusement, exactly. If Carlos had to guess, he would describe it as a proud smile.

"That is a very good trick, son," the king said. "A very good trick, indeed."

And as he said it, King Carmine let out a small yet unmistakable chuckle.

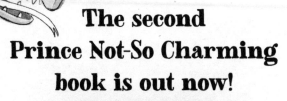

**The second
Prince Not-So Charming
book is out now!**

CHAPTER 1

"Whoa! Whoa!"

Prince Carlos Charles Charming could feel droplets of perspiration forming on his brow. He clenched his teeth. His eyes flashed with panic. His ankles began to shake.

"Whoooa!" he yelled.

Carlos's words bounced against the walls

of the empty ballroom, so as he yelled "whoooa," a bunch of *whoooas* yelled back at him.

It was a little disorienting. And now was *not* the time to be disoriented.

As Carlos *whoooa*-ed and wobbled, Jack the Jester sat crisscross applesauce upon a large purple velvet pillow. Jack nodded, making the bells on his red-and-green hat jingle-jangle.

Carlos found the jingle-jangling disorienting, too.

"You're doing fine, kiddo," Jack said. "Just relax. Just keep moving."

"I–I don't know if I *can* relax!" Carlos sputtered. "Every time I move, I . . . WHOA!"

"Whoa, whoa, whoa, whoa . . ." the walls replied.

It was as if Carlos was relearning how to walk, which was pretty much what he was doing.

"Let the stilts feel like part of your body," Jack instructed.

Weaving on his shaky stilts, Carlos blinked a drop of sweat out of his eye. "Is it hot in here?"

"That's fear sweat, boy," Jack said. "Don't worry. You're only three feet off the ground."

Carlos's feet may have been only three feet off the ground, but his head was *eight* feet off the ground. And it felt much, *much* higher.

Also, the feet at the end of his new, unsteady legs were not his normal size-nine shoes but two skinny poles no thicker than a silver dollar.

The very thought made him dizzy.

Don't think about it, don't think about it, don't think about it, Carlos thought.

But trying not to think about it made Carlos think about it even *more*.

"Don't lose focus," Jack warned.

But the sweat, tension, and dizziness made Carlos less focused than ever.

"Keep moving," Jack said.

Carlos took a step, but his stilt couldn't find the floor. He felt his weight shift. He felt himself fall. He caught a glimpse of the stone floor rushing up to meet his face.

PUH!

Oh! That fall was kind of pleasant, Carlos thought. *I didn't know stone floors could be so comfortable.*

He blinked once, then twice. He found his head resting on a large pillow made of purple velvet. His eyes flicked to where Jack the Jester sat, though Jack wasn't sitting anymore. He was on his feet, with his left arm outstretched before him, as if he had just released a bowling ball.

"Thanks for letting me borrow your pillow," Carlos said.

"Thanks for falling where I threw it!" Jack replied. "Your parents have enough problems with our jester lessons. I don't think they'd like it if I returned you to them with a dented head."

Carlos's parents, Carmine and Cora Charming, were the king and queen of the peaceful and happy land of Faraway Kingdom. That meant Carlos was a prince. That *also* meant that Carlos was expected to do princely things.

Jestering was pretty much the opposite of being princely, but Carlos loved it. And King Carmine and Queen Cora were good parents as well as good rulers. So they allowed the jester lessons to continue as long as jestering didn't interfere with Carlos's royal responsibilities.

Jestering, they told him, must only be a hobby. A very private, very *secret* hobby.

But jestering was more than a hobby to Carlos. It was his passion. And he was good at it, too. For the most part.

"You need a little more practice with the stilts, I see." Jack jingle-jangled over to where Carlos lay. He offered a hand, but Carlos didn't take it.

"Can I just lie here for a minute?" He was comfortable on the floor and still a little woozy.

"Sure." Jack smiled down at his student. "You earned a break. Would you like a little water?"

"Yes, thank you," Carlos said.

The flower on Jack's vest sprayed water in Carlos's face.

"HA-HA! Gotcha!" Jack wheezed with laughter.

Carlos dried his face on his sleeve and shook his head. *How did I fall for that old gag?* he thought.

Nonetheless, Carlos couldn't help but smile.

Jack plopped himself down on the stone floor. He was the only adult Carlos knew whose knees never made cracking noises. The jester scratched his chin and studied Carlos's face. "You do look a little glassy-eyed," he admitted. "Tell me a poop joke."

"Why?" Carlos asked.

"Poop jokes make the mind sharp," Jack said.

"They do?" Carlos asked.

Jack shrugged. "How should I know? I just wanna hear a poop joke."

"Okay . . ." Carlos tried to come up with a good one. "What do you call a fairy using the toilet?"

"What?" Jack asked.

"Stinker Bell."

Jack's brown cheeks stretched into a wide, merry grin. His dark eyes crinkled with delight. He let out a long, appreciative laugh. "That's a good one! You, kid, are a natural jester."

It was Jack's highest compliment, but Carlos couldn't fully accept it. "I don't know, Jack," he said. "I've been working with stilts for a month, and I still can't get the hang of them."

"You will," Jack assured him. "You got the hang of everything else."

This was true, but somehow stilt-walking was *different* from everything else. Every time Carlos got up on them, his eyes would get blurry and he'd start to shake. No matter how much he practiced, the feelings never went away.

"You're a fine jester, Carlos. And I'm not the only one who thinks so." Jack raised a mischievous eyebrow. "In fact, I have *news*."

Jack paused, letting the word *news* hang there for a moment to give it a little extra oomph. He peered over his shoulder. He lowered his voice. In Fancy Castle, spies could be anywhere. "Wanna work on your hobby in the village tonight?" he asked.

Carlos's eyes brightened. "You *know* I do," he whispered. "When, where, and what?"

"Five o'clock, Village Hall, the Zimmer-man bar mitzvah," Jack said.

Carlos's heart leapt. "Five o'clock. Hm. I think I can sneak out." His stilt-walking worries faded away. "One way or another, I *will* sneak out. I am *so* there."

Jack winked. "It'll be our little secret."

"And the Zimmermans' secret." Carlos winked back.

"And their fifty guests' secret." Jack chuckled.

"And the secret of the one hundred guests at last week's Stravini wedding." Carlos chuckled louder.

"And the secret of the thirty guests at

little Bobby Vapors's birthday party two weeks ago." Jack snorted.

"And the secret of everyone at the grand opening of Corky's Pre-Owned Catapults." Carlos snorted louder.

"And the secret of everyone at the annual Moat-Diggers' Convention!"

That's all we have room for, folks! But *Prince Not-So Charming: Her Royal Slyness* comes out alongside *Once Upon a Prank*. Look for it wherever books are sold!

ABOUT THE AUTHOR

Roy L. Hinuss is the authorized biographer of the Charming Royal Family. He is also fond of the occasional fart joke. When he isn't writing about Prince Carlos Charles Charming's many adventures, he can be found in his basement laboratory, making batches of homemade Brussels sprout ice cream.